THE NOT KEPT PROMISES

ARPITA M

ISBN 979-888629127-8

To those who inspires and will read.

Contents

Foreword

THE NOT KEPT PROMISES

(New adaptive changes of village girl to a big industrial city)

Myself Arpita manna being a pharmacist by profession. This story is my imaginary 1st story which is not being by you readers which is being publish. My no aim to harm any feelings it's just a short story of girl Radhika Mukherjee and boy Swapnashil Joshi. Where promises were done but one fails to keep it for life. Any copyright to this story is not applicable.

Other published work of mine was in book of quotes which were in Hindi language.

Hope you guys like my work.

CHAPTER ONE

A girl from small town of Kokalta named Radhika Mukherjee used to live her life in a very simple way. But her dreams to became a famous fashion designer was living which made her to live few more years. Her father Mr. Mukherjee was not letting to study further as in village the importance of studies, the importance to women talent was not considered. But Radhika's mother was much supportive to her.

Whenever she used to talk about studies or go out and work her father used to get angry.

It was seven o'clock in the evening in the clock, so Mrs. Mukherjee called Radhika to help in her household chores. As her mother let her used to concentrate Radhika in her designing sessions when Mr. Mukherjee was not around.

But That day Radhika and her mother gossiping some new ideas of designing which Mr. Mukherjee came to heard and started shouting on both. His temper was so high that it was out of control that he shouted "GET OUT OF MY HOUSE" you both.

Mr. Mukherjee "after denying so many times you still want to do same"
"GO GET OUT OF MY HOUSE"

Both crying and taking a pair of clothes and some daily needs moved out of house.

Now Mrs. Mukherjee asking Radhika what they will do where they will go?

Radhika replied "it's too late for let's spend tonight in near "dhaba" on highway which was 15 minutes away from their place. So, Radhika and her mom went to that dhaba. The men on dhaba knew Radhika as she used to help them whenever their family need her. Also, Radhika used to teach and play with their childrens which used to make a different environment for them as well as for customers.

Next day, now the night passes away but the question remains same "Where do we go ? What we will do ? "

Radhika was thinking now what she can do but nothing was striking her mind. Then a voice came Naya Bazaar!!!! Naya Bazaar !!!! from bus conductor suddenly the Radhika exclaimed " Yes, we can go to Naya Bazaar"

I know few people their. But again her mother asked

How ? we don't have that money.

Radhika replied I have some.

Mom " This is not enough, My dear"

Dhaba uncle " I can help you both"

Radhika "But ..."

Dhaba uncle " why girl when you used to help me have I ever stopped you ? Now my turn "

They borrowed some money from him and quickly catched up the bus.

It was a two hour drive from Radhika's village to Naya Bazaar. After a long route they reached to their destination. Again

Mrs. Mukherjee " This seems big city Radhika"

"How we will manage ?"

Radhika " relax mom"

"Now see how talented and ambitious your daughter is"

(Radhika used to come to Naya Bazaar to have a look for design and new pattern in market. So she knews many people and every part of the city. But her mom was not aware of this as everytime she used to lie her.)

In new market when similar faces came they shouted " Didi, Bohot din baad" in hindi

And her mom was shocked she knew half of the market

Radhika laughing !!

So now again Radhika mind started brain-storming....

Their he met his sir under whom she was learning designing. She told everything to him and explained how she is thinking to start her new life in new city. Her sir told " don't worry dear, I'hv my house which is closed, so you guys settle their"

Sir " don't worry I'll take rent charge from you"

" Okay Radhika"

Radhika (laughing) "Okay sir"

Radhika "let's go mom, I'hv few other works to complete"

Mom " okay beta"

they took a rickshaw and went to the sir's house.

CHAPTER TWO

(It was a new day with new beginning of their life.)

Radhika and her mom wake up early as per they daily schedule.

Radhika's mom " dear now how we will survive"

Radhika "mom we both are working from tomorrow" so now we both will earn and live our life.

Radhika "mom today we have to set our new house do some shopping"

" from tomorrow we won't get time to do extra chores"

Mrs. Mukherjee "okay beta, let's have a breakfast first then we will proceed"

(They both are having a breakfast sitting in their balcony, as the house is on 1st floor. But suddenly Radhika mom got stumbed thinking about Mr. Mukherjee. Radhika – "what happened mom ?"

Mom "thinking how your father would survive"

"Have he had his breakfast ?"

Radhika "mom this is his punishment only" (angrily)

Mom " no beta, you should not say this way"

Radhika gets up angrily and just exclaimed "mom, we need to complete many works by today, so get ready"

They both head towards city to buy their grocery, clothes and some other stuff for house.

But now they don't have enough money as they notice the price are too high for every single thing. They both again sat on the bench as they were near a park.

(Communication between Radhika and her mother started)

Radhika "mom this money is not sufficient"

Mother " yes beta"

Mother "you saw how costly things are"

Radhika "yes mom, so now ?"

(they both are thinking)

Mom suddenly saw her bangles and an idea blink in her mind

Mother "beta, why not we sell this bangles ?"

Mother "this will get us a sufficient money"

Radhika " but ...... um.... Mom"

Mom "No, but .... Nd all "

Mom "come'on let's go"

(they sold the bangles and started shopping their needs)

All stuff was collected from the market and the time on the clock tower was 7:00 PM

Radhika "mom we are tired, and see it's evening"

"Now what for lunch ?"

Mom "I'll cook, you are tired not me"

Radhika "A big No, mom"

Radhika "let's enjoy, we got new life from today so why not parcel some food"

Mom "Okay beta,"

(they both pick some ready packed food and move towards their apartment and have their meal. After completing household works they go to sleep.)

NEXT DAY

Radhika "mom fast we'r getting late"

"we have to catch up bus on time"

Mom "take your lunch, I've packed it"

They both left the house Radhika 1st took her mom to work place as she was quite new. Radhika's mom started working in a clothing industry where they have to stitched clothes as per orders. After leaving her mom she moved towards her work place. It was just 10 min of walking distance. The whole day passes away and in evening Radhika went to pick up her mom. Then from their they headed towards their apartment.

Mom got freshen up and started cooking for both of them whereas on the other side Radhika took after the other household works such as cleaning, organizing stuff which they bought yesterday and all other works.

As the dinner was ready mother called Radhika. With the dinner their gossips of whole day story started and when the dinner ended they didn't knew. After completing their after dinner works they moved to their cozy bed and slept with a quick relief.

Days and days passes away. Nor they remember their past nor Mr. Mukherjee ever came to contact them. They both were happy and now Radhika was also mature and grown up girl. So her mother also used to teas her

" When will you get marry now ?"

And Radhika always used to side away the topic by distrupting it with other gossips.

One day Radhika exclaimed " Mom, did you know, we are completing one year of our new life"

"celebration is necessary"

Then they planned a dinner in restaurant in evening after works and all the gossips moving to their workplace started.

Radhika arranged a beautiful night for herself and her mother.

When she was serving food from counter to her mother, she clash up a 5 feet, black brown hair, black small eyes guy wearing a denim jeans and light blue tshirt. They both said sorry quickly to eachother and moved towards their ways.

Again after a few minute Radhika and the 5 feet guy's eye met as the blue tshirt was sitting alone in the opposite direction of Radhika. Radhika saw that he is upset and is sitting alone so she and her mom went to that table.

Radhika "hello, Hope you don't mind if we sit here"

Boy "No, not at all"

Radhika to boy "have you ordered something ?"

Boy "No, not yet, wait we'll have it"

Waiter "Yes sir, How may I help you"

Boy "just note down our order"

And he gave a order of food for which now three of them are waiting. Meanwhile Radhika started a communication with the boy. Her mom is just trying to read Radhika's mind what is going in her head.

Radhika to boy "see it's not good that I call you by blue tshirt or 5 feet, So how may I represent you"

Boy "did I told you 4.5 feet or yellow kurti"

Boy "represent me as Sir, that's enough"

Radhika "but what mom calls you ? Sir ?"

Boy "Okay aunty, you may call me Swapnashil"

"swapnashil Joshi"

Radhika "ohhh.... My one friend is also Joshi, you guys have yummy food."

Radhika "why are you here in such a restaurant, sit home and enjoy food made by mom"

Swapnashil "Not everyone has a mother !!!!! (slowly whispered)

Radhika " what ?"

Swapnashil "Nothing"

Radhika "Do you live alone"

Swapnashil "Does it make sense to you ?"

Radhika " Actually No......, but see food is yet to come and you are not asking me so I thought to take interview you only"

Radhika mother " laughs very loudly"

Radhika "shocked to her mother"

Swapnashil "sorry aunty if I looks like stupid, but I'm getting irritated from your girl"

Radhika "Okay sorry man"

Swapnashil "it's okay"

Radhika "Hey can you help me, that juice centre looks amazing lets have some for three of us"

Swapnashil "Okay come'on"

They both headed towards the juice centre but as soon as they moved the table Radhika asked "what happened, is every thing alright ?"

Swapnashil "Can we sit here and talk for a minute ?"

Radhika "why not !! come"

They both sat on the table near juice centre. From the back Radhika mother is watching but she was knowing that something is wrong so she doesn't feel important to interrupt them.

Swapnashil "Boss fire employees from the office but I got fired from my home only" (in sad mood)

Radhika "could you elaborate so let's see if can help"

Swapnashil "yesterday I lost my job and I have borrowed some money also which they want right now, so the guys came home and papa came to know everything as I was lying them about my job also."

Swapnashil "They told you either bring money or leave this house as they don't people ask money on their door"

Swapnashil " even they told every family member not to help me. Because I belong to joint and my all brothers and sisters are well settle in or out of India. So my father feels shameful when they see me like this.)

Radhika " so basically your and mine story is same"

Radhika in hindi "Ha toda masala upper niche hai par story and life same hai"

Radhika "you know why me and mom are here today ?"

Swapnashil " No"

Radhika (laughs) "obviously no, we are celebrating 1 year of new life"

Swapnashil " 1 year of new life, Means !!!!!"

Radhika "I'm from a small village about 460 km away from this Naya Bazaar, my father doesnot like that I study and my dream is to become a fashion designer. Though I was pursuing designing course which was hidden from my dad. But one evening me and my mom were discussing about the new ideas of designing. Which my came to know and he thrown out of the house both of us."

Radhika "so today it's one year to us"

Swapnashil "from where you girls bring so courage"

Radhika laughs

Radhika "you too have same courage, its just today you are sad so cann't see it"

Radhika "to see such courage you ha▉ to be happy, which you cann't be (laughs and coughs)"

Swapnashil "how dare you to say like that (in angry face)"

Radhika "so where are living right now ?"

Swapnashil "no place because everyone knows me and father had warned everyone to help me"

Radhika "ohhh......ummm... well.. I've a plan, come let's go to mom"

Radhika to her mother "Mom can we make one help to Swapnashil ?"

Mother "What ?"

Radhika "can we share our apartment with him ?"

Mother "If you it is right, then okay no problem ?"

Swapnashil "No, this is not done, I'll figure out something"

Radhika "What sleeping on bench ?"

Swapnashil "Yes, that's the best idea !!!!"

Radhika "Are you mad or what "

swapnashil "you might be thinking but I'm not"

Radhika "keep your mouth shut and follow with us, until you don't figure out something comfortable"

Swapnashil "Aunty thank you so much"

(Three of them had their dinner and they celebrated even more beautifully. After completing their dinner they moved towards their apartment with a long walk and some funny gossips.)

Next day Radhika and her mom had to moved for their office but swapnashil was jobless and sad again Radhika taunt "Hello Mr., what are you thinking ? take rest today. I will talk to my sir and you will have your job tomorrow."

Saying this Radhika and her mom moved out of the apartment.

Swapnashil gets freshen up and searching for some jobs in newspaper. Meanwhile looking the apartment he got an idea to decorate and organizes the flat.

The whole day of swapnashil passed away in house works and when he sat on the couch he notice its time for mother- daughter duo to come. So he got freshen up and prepared a meal for dinner.

Radhika and her mother came and rang the bell. Swapnashil opens the door. They both got shocked after seeing the apartment. Those old curtains but decorated in antique way. Those sofa were old but their position to window make mood more beautiful. That side coffee table looks amazing in middle. Reshiftting that plants makes a cozy look to night mood.

After seeing this Radhika appreciated swapnashil and motivated him to work as a interior designer.

Mrs. Mukherjee heading towards kitchen to preapare meal but get shocked as it was also preapare.

Swapnashil "today no work, every thing is done"

Swapnashil plays a pleasant music and three of them sits and enjoy dinner with some funny tantrums and gossips.

Radhika "Okay so from tomorrow you won't get to do such works, because you have to work in my store"

All three of them were happy and enjoy their dinner.

Days passed and the three of started living happily.

Radhika and Swapnashil started bonding a beautiful friendship where they fights were less and gossips were more. Also their workplace being a same they used to share everything. Radhika's mother was happy as she got a relief that Radhika is becoming friendly with someone.

Now after dinner talks and household chores were also completed together. So when Radhika and Swapnashil finish their work they used to have coffee.

One beautiful evening, it was a full moon where both can see moon straight from the chair from their balcony. Holding a cup of coffee in hand

Swapnashil expelled out "What I would be if you haven't met me that day"

Radhika (teasing him) "Yes definitely, actually which bench number it would be ?"

Swapnashil (flirting with eyes)

Swapnashil "thanks yaar"

Radhika "ohh… today is memorable day, we became official friends "yaar""

Swapnashil laughs "How you pretend to be so funny"

Radhika "Hello, I'm funny"

A sound of calling Radhika……Radhika…… came from the room. They both headed towards their room for sleep. Days are passing away and now Swapnashil is getting some feelings for Radhika. But his fear of losing friendship is more than being in relationship. So he remains quite.

It was again full moon, a hand with a cup of coffee and some stupid gossips of Radhika and Swapnashil. But this time swapnashil interrupted " I like you Radhika"

Radhika shocked

Radhika "What did you just say ?"

Swapanshil said " Yes you heard it right"

Radhika "Why but"

Swapnashil "How can Why be a question in this Radhika (whispers softly)"

Swapnashil "I can't do anything with this feelings"

Radhika "Okay don't think too much and don't stress yourself, what if I want to say something ….."

Swapnashil "I'm here to hear out to you only dear, say it…. I'm listening"

Radhika "well…. Ummmm…… I also like your company"

Swapanshil dancing

Radhika "wait… first listen, I like your company but I don't love"

Swapnashil "now what is this new you brought madam"

Radhika laughing loudly

Swapnashil "explained it madam"

Radhika "This means for now I also don't want to spend a single minute without you, but if you leave me I'll let you go.

Swapnashil "why would I leave you, duffer"

Radhika "because it happens one day you someone so much and very next day you leave them and settle with other"

Swapnashil "No, promise I won't leave you and mom (radhika's mother)"

Radhika "ooooo.... Cheesey boy, you already married to me and settled in your dreams."

Swapnashil feeling shy "Yes madam, so madam if your today's teasing have completed then can we proceed to our bed ?"

Radhika " Yes !! Yes !! other mom will let to know that we are awake till so late"

Both proceed to their room but still the gossips is not over. They starts chatting through emojis and text which is taking their friendship to new level. This continues and now more flirty chats and gossips teasing eachother, complaining to mom everything flies beautifully.

Now the day of celebration was. Yes it was Radhika's birthday. The day before the birthday Radhika's mother and swapnashil planned beautiful surprise for Radhika in house itself. And their were no one only three of them.

So now it's 12:00 a.m 19th July (Radhika's birthday) special thing was today also it was full moon. So swapnashil planned the birthday accordingly. At exact 12:00 a.m swapnashil silently moved to Radhika's room and handover the letter. As soon as Swapnashil try to leave Radhika's she wakes up. Without leaving the hand they both comes in balcony. Radhika can't wait and opens the letter.

(The letter ---- Hey Radhika Happy birthday, may we celebrate each and every birthday of yours like this. But this is special note for all that birthday to be celebrated like this. Remember that full moon night we two, two cups of coffee, cozy summer winds and MY PROPOSAL. So today at your birthday I'm waiting for the answer of that proposal. Yours loving, 5 feet, blue tshirt Swapnashil.)

Radhika (laughing and crying)

Swapnashil "Now what happen? Do you want me to make some coffee ?"

Radhika "No duffer"

Radhika "You love me so much ?"

Swapnashil "Why you don't me"

Radhika teasing "No not this much"

Swapanshil (gets sad) "Okay lets sleep now, HAPPY BIRTHDAY "

Radhika "So you don't want answer to this letter ?"

Swapnashil "yes I want"

Radhika "Now or at night under full moon ?"

Swapanshil "It's all up to you, my dear, I can wait as long as you want"

Radhika starts crying . Swapnashil wiping tears coming more closure making a comfortable environment for eachother to talk.

Radhika "I love you duffer" crying

Swapnashil "But why are you crying" relaxing her by kissing on her forehead

Radhika tightly hugs Swapnashil

After few minutes both heads towards their room.

It was Radhika's birthday and the day even started beautifully. So Radhika decided to take a leave at her job. But their were planning which Swapnashil and mom decided to do. Now the change in plan was for sometime Swapnashil will take out Radhika outside and for sometime mom will take her out. So mom made some outdoor chores excuses and took her which in afternoon was took by Swapanashil.

In evening when Radhika entered with Swapnashil she was shocked after watching decoration. In th meantime mom exclaimed "this is all done by Swapnashil itself"

Radhika "thank you so much for this beautiful surprise" Swapanshil whispers "Anything for you, my love"

Now the three of them cut cake plays romantic songs with a dance of Radhika and Swapnashil. Have dinner which was came from their first meet restaurant. And the beautiful memorable day of Radhika and swapnashil came to an end at sleep.

After that Radhika and Swapnashil started behaving more like couples than friends. This was observed by Mrs. Mukherjee. So one day at dinner her mom asked "are you two liking eachother ?"

Both were silent

Mom "What should I consider for this silence ?"

Radhika " Mom......umm...."

Mom "Radhika, no umm.. a...., come to point Yes or No ?"

Radhika "Yes "

A complete silence in the house

Mom "you duffer guys why didn't you tell me earlier ?" Swapnashil "aunty...... we want but........."

Mom "wait.... So now whats the plan for future ?"

Swapnashil "marriage and family"

Mom "see Radhika you are lucky you have such a nice guy"

Radhika "yes mom I'm" seeing towards Swapnashil

Mom "I would make your life till marriage but why not you guys have engagement"

Radhika and Swapnashil both shouted YES

Mom in hindi "ohh my god.. itni jaldi thi to pehle kyu nai bataya"

After few days mom see a good muharat and Radhika-Swapnashill have their enagegment in complete rituals.

After a ritual completes a phone call comes to Swapnashil.

CHAPTER THREE

A phone call after rituals at Swapnashil cell is of his best friend Kartik where he tells Swapnashil to come home. His father is no angrier on him. But Swapnashil tells Kartik to tell his family not to interfere his life anymore.

Listening this Radhika gets angry as she doesn't like this tone of Swapnashil. She explains they are your family and you are today because of them only.

Swapnashil "No, today I'm because of you and you are only my family.

Radhika "yes we are family my love, but they are also"

Radhika "they are calling you might there be something, go once and see"

Swapnashil "at one cost "

Radhika "What?"

Swapnashil "you have to come with me"

Radhika "umm...."

Swapnashil "then I'm not going"

Radhika "let me 1st complete my answer"

Swapnashil "okay say"

Radhika "okay I'll but I should not become interference between you and your family."

Swapnashil "you won't, and we will talk about each other"

Radhika "okay, when we are going, we have to take leave from office"

Swapnashil "will let you know"

Radhika "let's have some food, you might be hungry"

They both have their food with mom. After that heading towards for washing dishes and completing their incomplete talks. As per their daily schedule they sit in balcony with a cup of coffee and some gossips.

After a week Swapnashil took Radhika at his place to meet and talk about their future. They were welcomed warmly after which snacks and then lunch were also offered. Radhika was a small village girl and she never seen such a huge mansion. But Swapnashil was always with her, holding her hand to show support she has.

Lunch was over and now they were sitting in a ballroom where the family members usually gathers after lunch and dinner. Swapnashil getting up from the couch gathering himself in the centre of room announced to gathers others members of the house.

(As womens were in kitchen and other household works)

Everyone gathered.

Swapnashil "Papa I want to tell something"

His dad "Yes, beta say it"

Swapnashil "This is Radhika. She is the one wo gave me home when I was thrown out."

His dad ".... Thanks beta (to Radhika) we had made a huge mistake by not trusting our son, but you did. Thanks a lot dear."

Swapnashil "Dad.. I want to say something"

Dad "Yes say"

Swapnashil "we love eachother and want to get married"

Dad "Okay, you children have decided then what can I say"

Dad "So now where you guys live"

Radhika "Florence apartment, 15 minutes of distance from Naya Bazaar"

Dad "okay" and few questions to Radhika about family to which she calmy replies to all questions.

Later on they both leave.

After a month, one day Radhika left the office a bit earlier informing Swapnashil as she was having some stuff to collect from the market for office as well as for house. In returning she called mom to ask if anything more she want for home.

Because now mother used to be at home only looking after all house works.

When Swapnashil returned he asked mom for Radhika. Mom replied that she haven't arrived might be late in traffic.

They both waited for Radhika but now its 9:00 p.m. they know that is not such careless girl.

Swapnashil continuously calling on Radhika's cell. No answer from the other side of the phone.

(Tense situation is becoming more worse.)

Swapnashil move out of the house to look for Radhika. Searching here and there. It was late and many shops were closed till by. After three hours of search someone responded.

Stranger "I saw this girl sitting in car"

Swapnashil "which car ? how does it look like ? have you seen the car number ?"

Stranger "as this street has less light focus, I can't see the number"

Stranger "but yes, their was a tiger face on back glass of the car"

Swapnashil "tiger face !!!"

Stranger " yes"

Swapnashil "okay thanks so much for help"
Swapnashil thinking that only his family know about the place they live and he has a car too which has a tiger face at back of glass. He exclaimed "Radhika kidnapped by my family, but why?"

As it was late night so no transporation was available to his home. So he decided to visit early morning.

The next morning when Swapnashil and Radhika mom went to Swapnashil house they saw Radhika hanging in their balcony.

SHOCKED

Radhika's mom shouting from ground Radhika..... Radhika..... Radhika....but Radhika was unconscious.
Swapnashil ran quickly making his way to balcony but the security his kept was strong enough. Swapnashil just only could see Radhika's face and not any thing else. Hence he started fighting back with the security. Before he can reach to the balcony his father cut the rope which was attached to Radhika.

Radhika fell down with a head injury. Blood all over the floor . Which made Swapnashil and her mom got stumbled.

Immediately a ambulance was called by Swapnashil and they went to hospital.

By Dr. words it was a very critical condition. Internal damage and due heavy blood flow Radhika was fighting between death and life. Swapnashil was in contact with doctors and medical team so that Radhika gets in stable condition as soon as possible.

After eight hours of wait a relief words came out from doctors.

"she is out of danger, but......."

Swapnashil "but..... what ?"

Dr "she is in coma, no one when she will comes out of it"

Swapnashil "starts crying"

Dr "see she can hear you, its just her body is not responding, go talk to her"

Swapnashil running towards ward "Hey duffer, so this is what promises are"

"are you going to keep your promises this way ?"

"This way I can marry you, See you sleeping on bed"

"and every household work I have to do, this is not fare"

"your blue tshirt wasnts to listen you"

"are you making your orders or I should move out of the ward"

Swapnashil was just asking questions and questions and crying but their was no reply from Radhika.

Moving out of the ward a noise came S.....S....Swa.......Swa.....

Swapnashil suddenly moved backward. He observed their were some movements but not perfect. He called doctor, doctor examined Radhika where they told to Swapnashil that she is in coma she can't answer you.

Swapnashil tried to explained to doctor but suddenly nurse calls doctor for another emergency patient and he has to run away.

Swapnashil knows that for few seconds Radhika called him. But no was ready to believe him.

Days and days passes away in hospital. Swapnashil every used to shout on Radhika to get up and speak up but Radhika was not replying to him. Months also passes but the situation of Radhika was same.

One day when Swapnashil decided that today he is going to scold Radhika very much. When he visit to the ward the Radhika was on same bed same machines were working as routine Swapnashil sat on the table hold Radhika's hand and he was just going to start scoulding to her when she hold his hand. Swapnashil has to pinch himself this time before calling to doctor.

But yes Radhika was responding and so she has holded his hand. Swapnashil called the doctor suddenly saying this time I'm not joking. Doctor examined Radhika and were shocked to see the results. Slowly slowly Radhika started to say words.

Radhika "hello Dr"

Radhika "Dr you we are best friends, we have same story, so we live togther"

Radhika "Dr one can that we are not couples"

This sentence make a silence in Swapnashil soul.

After the again examination of Radhika it came to a note that she doesn't remember anything of last five -six months. (So now Swapnashil had to make sure that this relationship tag won't make any stress to Radhika. As this is the cruiel stage still to her life.

After two days of under examination Radhika was given discharge from hospital.

Three of again started living happily just the difference was Swapnashil has to calm his soul very much. And always had to pretend fake infront of her Radhika. But he managed to do this so well.

Again Kartik, Swapnashil's best friend called him to come back home and his answer was the same "tell them that I died."

Happy days were again flowing in Florence apartment. And this time its was Swapnashil's birthday. He planned the same situation as that was back on radhika's birthday.

The answer was same to him on the birthday and again they get bonded in beautiful relationship.

CHAPTER FOUR

CHAPTER FOUR

Swapanshil proposed Radhika and Radhika said yes. But this time Swapnashil decided to move out to new place as he has the fear of repeating the past.

Somehow, he manipulated and convinced Radhika to move to north of India as he knows one of his friends there who can help them to settle their. They started packing the stuff and before leaving the town Swapnashil make sure that the Radhika's treatment is completed for which he contacted the doctor of the town as well as Delhi.

In few days they shifted to Delhi, where Swapnashil met his old friend who helped them to settle down in the city. His friend also helped him to get a high package job.

The three of them were settle and adaptive with the new environment.

Months passes away and now Radhika is alright. She was ideally sitting at home and browsing the internet. The internet pages show a scholarship application page from abroad university for fashion designing.

On page it was mentioned that it is online course. So Radhika filled up the form. She didn't inform this to Swapnashil.

Few weeks passed away early morning Radhika got up a popup on her phone. She opened it. It was the email, the response from UK university of her scholarship.

Yes she got scholarship to study at one of the finest UK university.

Swapnashil was sleeping in the bedroom

Radhika went running to bedroom and waking him up.

Radhika "wake up love, see I got scholarship to study at UK university"

Swapnashil " UK university? When did you fill form?"

Radhika "few weeks back. When I was sitting ideal at home"

Swapnashil "congrats my love" kissing her forehead, hugging her tightly and excitedly.

Swapnashil " so what's the next process?"

Radhika "nothing much just a visa application"

Swapnashil "that's wonderful, I know my one friend who can help us in this"

"I'll call him just you get me your documents"

They started processing the file and moving to UK. But now only one person can go with Radhika. So again the silence move in house as they can't live mother alone nor Radhika and Swapnashil live separated.

Next second mother exclaimed you guys worry a lot.

Mother "see I won't to live their you guys go and have settle their"

Mother "I'll join you guys afterwards"

Swapnashil "but.... Mom..."

Mother "you both have a bad habit of BUT...."

Mother "follow my orders."

Swapnashil "okay mom"

Radhika and Swapnashil started their packing. Swapnashil has to go Delhi embassy to collect their passport and visa. As Radhika was busy Swapnashil alone move to collect the documents.

By returning to home from Delhi Swapnashil met with a serious accident.

A call came at Radhika's cell that "the person whose phone belongs has met with an accident, we are taking him to the city hospital please come over their"

Listening this Radhika runs to city hospital. She doesnot know much about the city but manages to reach the hospital. Her mom doesn't know anything as she have been went to market.

After one hour of hospitalization doctors informs Radhika that Swapnashil is death.

Radhika went to ward and shouts at Swapnashil

"so this is your promise to me"

"you duffer I don't like this type of mischief"

"get up otherwise you'll have do all household chores every day"

"that would be your punishment you 6 feet"

Nurses trying to handle Radhika

But she is saying only one thing "I was also serious few months back but I came, and see him he hasn't kept his promises"

Radhika "hey you, yes you, Mr. Swapnashil Joshi where is your PROMISE to not leave me alone"

After Swapnashil's death Radhika again applied to UK university as it was now Swapnashil's effort and dream which she has to fulfilled. So she went to UK with her mom. She lived her entire life in the memory of Swapnashil. Her mom is to explain her to live life happily but there she was. She was living the life not for happiness but to complete her breath.